WE PLAY HERE

WE PLAY HERE
Dawn Watson

GRANTA

Granta Trust, 12 Addison Avenue, London W11 4QR

First published in Great Britain by Granta Poetry, 2023

Text and drawings copyright © Dawn Watson, 2023

A CIP catalogue record for this book is available from
the British Library.

10 9 8 7 6 5 4 3 2 1

ISBN 978 1 91505 106 6
eISBN 978 1 91505 107 3

Typeset in Minion by Hamish Ironside

Printed and bound in Great Britain by T J Books, Padstow

www.granta.com

It's that night now. Like a boy with a Hallowe'en sparkler, he draws on the dark with a lit cigarette. The words are ghosted from his mouth in plumes and wisps of smoke, as I hold his free hand to guide him through the story, and we walk its underworld again.

– CIARAN CARSON, *The Star Factory*, 1997

I never had any friends later on like the ones I had when I was twelve. Jesus, did you?

– STEPHEN KING, 'The Body', 1982

CONTENTS

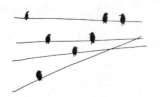

Summer 1988

There are four of us: Nell, Sam, Max and me.
I'm Ellen. We're twelve, except for Max,
who's eleven. Our gang is the Ghost Tigers.
At home, no one knows much about me.
My mum stays shut up in our dark lounge
and I stay shut up. Her smile is dark and bent.
My best friend Nell lives three doors up.
She broke her foot on a pommel horse
and was off school for three whole months.
She rode her bike in a cast, hip-to-toe.
Her dad was a very tall hospital nurse.
He died of cancer he caught in the ER.
Then Sam lives in a flat over the road.
At Easter, her dad was hanging from a tree
but is OK. In a photo of Sam on her wall
she's a baby on a stool in the Somerton Inn.
Her dad is out of focus, lighting a cigarette.
Max is our leader and lives in the next street.
If you go by her house, you hear her dad
hit her and her mum. It's just the vacuum
blattering the walls, Max says. Her house
has a CCTV camera sticking on the wall.
Her dad is important and scares people.
Their bay window is covered in big circles
of dry Windolene so no one sees in or out.

NELL

Queen of the Sticklebacks

It was midsummer and everything concrete
was a river. Pavement slabs rippled like shallows.
Painted kerbs were odd fish strung in a line:
red, blue and white, red, white and blue.
The water ran low as a bath, turning quick
into a pocked road, moss green and silt plumbed.
The raised alleyway was a stubborn dyke
that saved me daily. Or it seemed that way.
Things weren't really covered in water.
But it made me feel like I'm on a pike boat
held safe over the top of things. I knew better,
and sometimes I saw Belfast as it is:
dry and full of threat. But that was harder.
Just to see what would happen, I put one foot
on each white entry post and dared the river
to overwhelm me. Come on, I said. Rise up, sure.
Carry me out of here. But the posts did their job.
There was no messing about on this occasion
from footpaths in north Belfast trying to flood
their banks. The front yard walls stayed put,
hedges held fast, and greened telephone poles
curbed the tarmac flood plains quietly.

Two boys waded up Ashfield Gardens, one ginger,
one blond. Blond in a blue tracksuit, ginger in red.
Both pairs of trousers were ripped from the knees
to the ankle bones. Tiny sticklebacks smacked
their lips in the holes. Blue shouted, Are you a boy
or a girl? He had a ragged cleft lip. I'm a girl, I said.
You're wearing boys' clothes. So? I shrugged.
So, looks shite, yelled Red. They're second-hand.
My face flushed. A dustbin rushed past in a current.
The boys started singing, Hurrah! Hurrah!
We are the Billy Boys. I'd never heard Catholics
sing it. The spooked fish shut their mouths.

Why are you singing that if you aren't Protestant?
I said. Red laughed. Blue gasped, then shouted,
What's a Protestant? I admitted I didn't know.
They ducked under the water and resurfaced
with handfuls of smooth worn rock and brick.
We can only be nice if you give us your skateboard.
Red threw a stone and it hit me on the eyebrow.
I gripped the green board in front of my face.
Blood ran into my eye, trickled warm on my lips.
The boys splashed towards me in goose-steps,
synchronised, and snatched it from my hands.
The board said, Skate and destroy, in fire letters.
My blood plip-plopped in the swelling river.

Red and Blue had lived in the area six months.
They had worn the same tracksuits every day
since they moved in. They arrived after an army
of Housing Executive builders wearing rain slickers
built a dead-end string of houses at the bottom
of our street. It used to be a patch of wasteland
backing onto Dunmore greyhound track.
People built bonfires down there every July
out of tyres and sofas. The builders whizzed diggers
and cement mixers in on inflatable dinghies.
They extended Ashfield Gardens into something
shaped like a thermometer: the long street leading
to a mercury glob of houses boiling at the end.

The people the Housing Executive moved in
had one route in and one route out: my street.
The people the Housing Executive moved in
were Catholics, which was shocking and exotic.
They had no money, and we had no money.
There was a pocked patch of untouched tarmac
between where the old Ashfield Gardens ended
and the new one began. There sat my alley.
It was dry and dark, tucked under a lamp post.
Everything else had turned to water.

Last month, the Executive pulled a fast one.
Everyone in our street was told to move.
Builders returned in skipjacks, dropping anchor
at the post box to implement their grand plan
of kitchen extensions, updates and renovations.
It was goodbye and goodnight to everyone's homes
and wallpapers and door handles and carpets
and windows and fake tile linoleum. Overnight,
the people of Ashfield Gardens were exploded
like a stone tossed in a bucket of sticklebacks.
They had to go live in old and empty houses
on the opposite side of the stretched-out street
until the unexplained renovation was complete.
They were told it might take a year, or forever.

The Housing Executive, shiny in waders, reeled me,
my mum and my brothers out of number twelve
and dropped us in the holding tank of number three.
Old Elsie in number sixteen bit on a spinner lure
that must have looked like a Berkeley menthol
and ended up in the chum bucket of number five.
Luke, who was unmarried, alone and rumoured
to be a Catholic, was speared in number eight
and strung up in number nine. Angry Mrs Lowe
and the tall woman long assumed to be her sister
were netted in number twenty and released
in number one. Azra and her four grown-up sons
fell for luminescent stick bait in number ten
and got cut loose in number seven.

I spent the week of the Great Move watching
from my alley step. I picked wads of used gum off
the warm black ground and chewed up the last
of its gritty mint. I saw Luke on a wood pallet raft
towing fourteen ceramic animals to his new home
on the gable end. Two cream pugs were locked
in an illicit embrace, white Great Danes danced.
A tall clay duck was stunned to see a red wolf
crying in a cobalt plastic glitter collar.

They didn't see Azra wading across the road,
balancing five tomato plants in blown-glass bowls.
She wobbled on slick rocks pickled in algae.
Azra didn't see Elsie roll up her slacks to go ask
the man on the corner with the long black rifle
and combat boots if he wouldn't mind swimming
to the shop to get her ten Berkeley menthol.
Sorry love, I'm stood between you and a war,
he said. Elsie pressed her lips together in a line.
Three green Saracens floated up the main road.
No one saw Mrs Lowe gripping her sister's hand
and shivering, neck-deep in the clear blue water,
feeling for a sunken telephone chair with her feet.

I saw my mum and brothers sail to our new digs
in an upturned MFI wardrobe, using a yard brush
and curtain rails as barge poles. It was surprisingly
watertight for something made of laminated,
medium-intensity fibreboard. John and Mark
were crying and my mum was crying. She wailed,
But isn't it like this anyway, sure? Isn't it always
the same? Crows, displaced in the gathering flood
and looking for newly renovated nests themselves,
clacked beaks to confirm what she said was true.

The Housing Executive builders wore spacesuits
to tear down my bedroom walls. When he was alive,
before my parents split, my dad painted the walls
with every cartoon character he could think of.
He thought I'd like them better than wallpaper.
And I did. Pluto, Goofy and Mickey are quare smilers.
They smiled all day and all night, even when he died.
Even though they knew as well as I did my dad
would never be back to touch up Donald Duck's beak
when I accidentally tore his nostrils off with sticky tape.
The NASA builders piled up technicolour rubble.
There were bits of white feathers and red shorts,
buttons and a black circular ear dumped in a skip.
I watched while treading water.

North Belfast never used to be a whole river.
When I was small, it was a gutter trickle.
It started raining when my uncle knocked our door
in late November the year before. I answered,
and the orange-brown leaves got winched
off the trees by light that bent the branches.
He told me my dad had cancer in his liver.
I was told on the step he had two weeks to live.
It was like he said Billy Duddy's sweet shop
sold orangutans. It was like he said the leaves
on the trees were Maltesers. I lost the bap
a wee bit. I asked my uncle, What is a kohlrabi?
What is a romanesco? I laughed and laughed.
I stared at the ceiling with my mouth open.

Two days later in his Mount Vernon flat, high-rise,
I asked my dad if he hurt anywhere. Listen to me,
Nell, he said. Remember you are as good as anyone.
Don't let them tell you different. Have a geg, love.
Make sure to cut your hair as short as you want.
And tell your future girl I said look after you.
The rest of the afternoon, we watched Formula One.
I noticed the big black tyres were rippling.
He told me to choose a chocolate bar from a bag.
I took a Twix. The wrapper was wet in my hand.
The next day, my dad was dead.

Last summer, I stood on a chair as he taught me to gut
pike we caught in a secret lake, the slippery parcels
of innards snagged in rock-dark blood. He held the flesh
skin-side down in the frying pan with two wet fingers.
The fish bones struck a stern curve on the worktop.
He said, Very good job, Nell. Watch that wee knife.

They buried him on a Saturday. The big wake
was at my aunt's house on Skegoneill Avenue.
I saw his white face through a crack in the living
room door. The coffin floated to the hearse.
The crowd in Brantwood Football Club cheered.
Its blue metal turnstile creaked and whuppeted.
The marsh ground under the pallbearers' feet
was thick with flip-flop pike.

When the Great Move was finally over and done,
Ashfield Gardens closed its doors one by one.
From across the street came the clink and batter
of hammers and chisels. Metal sounds different
when it sings on water. Midges gathered in clouds.
My mum and brothers locked themselves inside
a room with purple chintz dragonfly wallpaper.
They were crying and my mum was crying.
She wailed, But isn't it like this anyway, sure?
Isn't it always the same? I grabbed my BMX.

It's not easy to ride in a river, lake or sea.
I headed to Grove Park, wobbling on mud banks
slanted beneath hedges and bolted garden gates.
Green Saracen turrets peeped out of the water.
On the corner, the man with the long black rifle
and combat boots. Lonely Luke's white ceramic
dogs. When my bike's blue tyres spun in silt,
I planted my left foot among discarded cans,
stones and metal bed frames. I climbed off
to push in patches. I crossed Skegoneill Drive
on pallets stretched between boulders.
I crossed Jellicoe Avenue on a fallen silver birch.
The park's green railings stretched for miles.
Its wrought-iron points wriggled above the water.
I got off my bike and squeezed it through a gap.

The grass river stretched wide to the horizon,
to the crest of a hill where the water thinned.
Rusted metal benches were sunk at angles.
Sycamore stood at the edge like stuck pins.
It was all sky and cold and river. I pushed
my bike to the top and stared out at the docks.
Fat cargo crates in pine green and ultramarine
were locked in a stare-down with the gantries.
I rang my bell to set its thin *cling-k* echoing
over the dark water, to the neck of the dry dock.

The tiny sticklebacks gathered at my feet.
When the river goes down, I whispered,
I will go and get my skateboard back.
I will punch those two boys in the face.
I won't be afraid. I'm as good as anyone.
I pedalled hard down the very steep hill
and the river welled behind me, a flood
of silver motes. I would wait on that bright
yellow crane for the waters to subside.
I would wait above the rivets and slipways
where everything smells like honeysuckle.

MAX

The Starlings of Dunmore
Died on the Eleventh of July

I heard them hit the ground like pound coins falling out of trouser pockets. They must have followed me home from Alexandra Park.

The noise woke me. I tottered to the window on stilts,
scanning the street for the source of the dings and stints.
Night was too hot and light for ten o'clock, even in July.
I pressed my forehead to the glass. My skin made a halo.
Outside, the dented street light was orange and fizzing.
The entry's white-painted posts were peeler blue.
Ruptured footpath slabs cast tooth shadows off kerbs
and cracks along Skegoneill Drive. Black was thrown
in all directions. I couldn't see to the bottom of the street,
even with my cheek to the pane. I knew it was the birds.

I had spent the day in the park. I'd looked at the food
in Crazy Prices on the Antrim Road until I got cold,
then cut down Jubilee Avenue to the vast entrance.
The four stone gate pillars are giant. Small, startled
flowers are carved into the rock. The whole shebang
is a fearful wasteland of bricks, rust, prongs and spikes,
lined with heavy sycamores. Alexandra Park carries
the smell of old graveyard badness about it. It tips up a hill
and falls away to the Protestant end. An interface tilts
over the strict white bridge into trees as stepped and steep
as the unsteady, brick-full stream slicing through it.

A couple of long summers back, wee Jim Harding fell off
the park's metal hexagon climbing frame onto concrete.
His leg broke under him with a sound like a crisp packet
getting stood on. His aunt ran over, sprung from the row
of big Victorian houses set like overbearing maths jotters
opposite the stone gateposts. Her mouth, fixed in a square,
emitted a weary yow-ow-ow. In a panic, our mate Sam
had tried to climb the hard green railings growing tall
out of thick border walls that forever pushed the park
below footpath level in its sunken north-east corner.
The railings had curved spikes like horns.

Today, I had obviously summoned the birds without thinking.
Clock seeds blew over patches of melted tarmac, gravel
and tin cans where fires were set, and settled in the park.
Not enough air, despite the cold sweeping down over
the houses from Divis mountain, where they crucified Jesus:
three vast TV transmitter masts like an Ulster Golgotha.
Green space left to be green when it shouldn't have been.
Trails from an inner perimeter weaving down to the path.
Invisible ways in and out, gaps. Handsome pan loaf bags
tied to the desperate railings round the lake. Paint peeling.
The flock of starlings hovering over the water.

I hid on the secret lane and spoke over the marsh reeds,
over the concrete dock, to the cloud of blattering wings.
I said to them, What are youse doin', what are youse doin',
what are youse doin'?

Later, I sallied out over the bridge to my granda's house
on the Limestone Road. I stayed for biscuits and juice
and accidentally pressed his red emergency fall alarm.
Hello, hello, said the ambulance man. I hoofed away on
to my aunt Emma's house in Mountcollyer.
You say it *Amma's*. She put a picnic blanket on me
on the settee and we watched *Catchphrase*. Every Eleventh,
she lit a kids' boney in the burnt-out Castleton playground
on York Road. Melted benches seemed more violent
than cheerful swings on fire with their bright metal strings.

On the way home, I cut past the park, up the worn, bent concrete steps to Gainsborough Drive. The iron banister has delicate, welded metal balls to stop you sliding down. You can see the docks from the top; Samson and Goliath, the gantry cranes, the old brown mill off the Shore Road, all unfolded and creased into life like a pop-up Bible.

Before I went to bed, Pat Loudon was in the living room
telling my mum to do the double. He was a drunk man
with a long dog called Tiny. He had a mole on his face
the colour of dirt. It moved up when he grinned,
like he was holding his teeth up for you to see.
I was told to make him tea. I'll poison him,
I decided. He was shouting, so was my mum.
I poured Brasso in the bottom of the cup.
He didn't notice and neither did she.

Now, the house was empty. I listened for rumble voices.
The *dada-dun-dun-dun* of 'Another One Bites the Dust'
had quit poking through the floor. Their party was over.
I pressed my big toe into my bedroom's red-pile carpet
which nearly sucked me under. On the walls, cut and stuck
pages from *Metal Hammer*, *Hit Parade* and *Kerrang!*
fill every space. Steve Harris was the ugly face of metal.
I slipped onto the landing, left my room lit by street light.

The stairs smelled of cigarettes. The toilet was gurgling.
The adults had spilled to the dogs. From down the street,
the tin crack of the dog trap in Dunmore Stadium came
spiralling through the open front door. I heard a faint cheer
and sensed the giddy crowds in the wooden stands alight.
It was a month before Toy Boy won the high-flown record
for the fastest dog of 1988. The race ground was sand,
like they were at the beach. The whole bright shebang
tumbled behind a tall green metal fence. From the street,
you could just about see the top of a gigantic floodlight.
A beautiful white blaze that didn't try to spill over.

Yesterday, I had woken in the night with a bang.
I jumped up, ran to the top of the stairs and sat down.
I gripped the banister at the blackened thumbprint
where the white gloss had been touched before it was dry.
The whorls and swirls gathered dirt. A clatter sprang
clean from downstairs. Do you want me to hit you?
said my dad. The yellowed skirting board was scuffed.
The paint was chipped off in the shape of Australia.
I moved halfway down the stairs. The living-room
door was wide open. My dad stood over my mum
with the poker. She was crouched between the settee
and the magazine rack. Her arms were fixed above
her head. She dropped them to whisper at my dad.
Her blonde hair was over to one side. He hit the poker
on the wall. She flinched her head towards her chest.
I leapt downstairs and jumped off the third last stair.
I ran in and my shoulders drew up to my ears.

He looked like the moon looks in the daytime.
Daddy, don't! My mum dropped her arms.
In a normal voice, like she would speak to the postman,
she said, John, stop, John. Maxine's up out of bed.
She waved like she was leaving. He dropped the poker.
He grabbed her hair and pulled her into the hall.
Her foot hit an empty Bacardi bottle and it rolled
under the settee. I said, Stop. My dad tried to drag
my mum upstairs. His curly hair was radioactive.
He shouted, You did, Jean. You know you did.
She kicked out at him, he fell back, then stood up
and walked to the kitchen. The back door slammed.
My mum touched her head as if it was impossible
she was real. Get out of the house, love, she said.
Run to the corner. There was blood on her brow
in the shape of a tired giraffe. I ran down the steps
and up the street.

Tonight, the street was orange and smelled of smoke.
All the people indoors on the phone to other people.
Telephone wires fritzed overhead, big news of damage
from street pyres, from peeler to Brit, and mum to dad,
and granny to aunt to neighbour. Did you see the fire
down the York Road, sure, someone would always say.
The swings would be melted. There were the ashy remains
of a digger on the corner of Ashfield Gardens
from a street party earlier. The bonfire was still lit
on top of a sheet of corrugated metal in the middle
of Glandore Parade. Nothing could get down it now.
It was a short street. I walked beneath the last sparks
of the bonfire. The rippled and patched concrete road
was a beanfeast of beer cans, beach chairs and ripped
burger buns. Sadie's gate creaked in number seven.
Blind Scruff barked. A late-season wasp circled
the shrunken black privets. The big light went out
in number three. Wee Jim's blue BMX was tangled
in plastic bunting. I used to borrow it when he let me.
Then his dad said, Get your own bike.

Skegoneill Drive dead-ends with the fence separating us from Dunmore Stadium. Underneath was a long dry bed of dirt about one foot high held up by a short brick wall. On the ground were two hundred dead starlings dropped out of the sky.

The birds were on car bonnets, on kerbs and on hedges.
There was a bird on a cheese-and-onion crisp packet.
There were about ten birds on Mrs Beggs's garden path.
There was one on a blue Cortina with an eye shut,
beak slack like it was looking through a telescope.

The birds were on the road. They were lying in patches
and curves and ones and twos and fours. Face down,
side down, all along the gutter. The dying bonfire
behind me was indifferent. All around, the starlings
were puffed up and pinched as though holding
their breath and wondering why help doesn't come
to small things.

I dug dirt graves under the fence with a lolly stick.
The racing traps went smack, slap-smack. Who cares?
I tell the birds, It's not your fault, it's theirs.
Their feet bones stuck up like RTÉ aerials,
wings crossed, eyes rolled back and open.

SAM

The Seaview 152

The Hatchet Man is gianter than you, said Tommy
Hillis. I believed him. He was outside Lou's corner
shop in Queen Victoria Gardens. It was half past eight
on Friday morning. But how giant exactly? I asked.
About this size, he said. The tip of his white Hi-Tec
sneaker touched the pebble-dash wall, fingers stretched
halfway up the window. I wrote *bigger than me*
in my notebook. He stood up and took a Mars Bar
from his pocket, opened it, threw the wrapper down.
It blew flat against the wall. Way gianter, he said,
and took a bite. I sketched the wall and the window,
drew a double-headed arrow in between. I wrote
hatchet diameter underneath. Tommy took off
down the alley towards Seaview Primary School,
which didn't have a view of the sea.

At break outside the toilets, a crowd of wee girls
skipped with a long blue rope. I leant on the red
brick wall and watched Janet Chowbury end a run
of eighty-four skips. She could skip far more than
Bridget Willets, who was celebrated for her skipping.
Janet owned two sausage dogs, both called Biscuit.
She joined Seaview Primary School last year in P6,
left east Belfast because her mum was told to.
Janet told me five times she missed her old best friend
Cheryl Dornan. Her uniform was navy, ours is grey.
Her mum made her wear it anyway. When she joined
the back of the skipping queue, I opened my book
and asked what she knew about the Hatchet Man.

Janet pushed her clear plastic glasses up her nose.
She said he kept it in the hedge. The hatchet? I asked.
Yes, she said. I frowned. What hedge? Front or back?
The yellow one, she said. I wrote, *Keeps his hatchet
in the front hedge.* A raindrop spat on a letter e,
the ink bled, the page would later go wavy.
I snapped the book shut and pinged its elastic twice.
Janet tugged at the waist of her blue pleated skirt.
Thanks for your help, I said. You were a good skipper
today. She squinted. Her mouth hung open slightly.

I ran around the back of the school, sat on the ground
beside the pitch. It took ninety-four steps. I liked it
was an even number. You had to count fast if you ran.
The grass was empty but for three blackbirds. No one
was allowed on it. I opened my book, drew the hedge.
It was overgrown, sagged in the middle. No one
had ever seen the Hatchet Man, but everyone knew
he lived almost exactly halfway down Seaview Drive.

His house was on the left coming from Premier Drive.
I walked past it every day to get to school. Everyone
made sure to stay on the right. People would tell you,
Stay on the right. On your own, you run fast past it.
The house was on a gable end, the hedge crept around
the side. It was patched in parts with wire fencing,
a yellow-splattered privet turning green at the back.
I wrote *hatchet kept here* with an asterisk. I tapped
the page with the pencil, tucked my hair behind my ear.
One of the blackbirds took off, landed on the goalpost.
I underlined *here* and turned the page. I fixed it flat
with a crease. The bell went for the end of break.
A dog outside the school gates barked my name.
It went, Sam Black- wood. Sam Black- wood.
I touched my neck eight times, put the notebook
in my denim backpack that had planets stitched on it.

After school, I went to Lou's to get a Curly Wurly.
I went there two times every day. If we needed bread,
my mum said, Go get a loaf, tell Lou to put it down.
If the shop was busy, I'd rejoin the queue at the back.
To make sure no one heard. At the till, Lou never spoke.
She would take her short pencil from behind her ear,
jot the bill in her book with the math-grid squares.
Then, she would look over my head at the next person.
Smile at them, Hello, take money for their milk,
beans, sausages, sticks, newspapers. The proper way.
Our tick list went over all the pages. It seemed to whistle
when Lou opened the book. I wondered if she was angry.
I was angry. Getting bread made my heart beat fast.

Janet Chowbury's sister Heather got a job in Lou's.
It meant she knew about the list. That made two people
apart from me, mum and dad. I set the Curly Wurly
on the counter. Heather flipped to our last tick entry,
scratched in the price of the chocolate with a pencil.
I counted twenty-six plastic tubs of sweets on the shelf.
Below, spilled fat mint Mojos; sharp beef Mini Chips
(vicious kindling moist with flavour); Skydiver crisps
with corn arms hoisted; booby-trap Puff Candy explodes
when bit; buff Highland Toffee bars stowed cold
and smacked into shards that scatter amber, cracked,
when the wrapper rips; Choc Lick dust to eat with fingers
sucked and dipped; salt and vinegar Skeleton Bones
to numb and peel your lips; a frozen cola Tip Top
to hack to slush with a stick; Pyramints are dear
and ambitious but will make you love Egyptology.
Nobody takes Rainbow Drops seriously but they last
a long time. Midget Gems, Black Jacks, Floral Gums,
Strawberry Bonbons, Chocolate Raisins, Chewing Nuts.
Without looking up, Heather said, Did you hear Henry
Rawley touched the Hatchet Man's door?

I had two whole pages on Henry in another notebook.
He once touched Shauna Langley's boobs in the park.
I sometimes imagined him kissing me and not asking.
He was wearing a Karate Kid lotus-flower sweatband
the day he got expelled from Castle High School
for hitting his teacher on the head with a typewriter.
His dad was jailed for killing a woman in the Waterworks.
She wasn't his girlfriend at the time but sometimes was.
He had four brothers and one died in a fight with a gang
on the Limestone Road over a half-full can of Coke
his granny gave him for helping her phone an ambulance
when her heart slowed down trying to open biscuits –
Blue Riband ones, which were the nicest.

I put the Curly Wurly in my pocket, took out my book.
When did he touch the door? Yesterday, she replied.
Was he seen? I asked. It was after school, she said.
Heather paused. Radio Ulster crackled behind her.
A woman in a green coat handed her the right money
for a Veda. We watched her leave. Heather continued.
Henry ran up the path for a dare and then at the door –
Heather straightened a box of 10p Mix-Ups with the tip
of her index finger. Then what happened? I whispered.
Well, said Heather, all the fucking windows opened.
They all flew up in a big slam. And the front door, too.
She rolled the pencil between her finger and thumb.
Her eyes were like Liquorice Wheels. A trap, she said.
Did the Hatchet Man come out? I asked. I wrote *trap*.
Lou shouted from the back for Heather to stock the milk.
She dropped the pencil. It was attached to a white string
and disappeared behind the counter. No, she said.
His eyes were black and his head reached the hall ceiling.
She picked up a blue crate of silver-topped bottles.
Hatchet was in his hand, she said. Blood all over it.
Henry ran like fuck. Heather sailed off down the shop.
When I opened the door to leave, a tiny bell jangled.

I lived a hundred and eleven steps away – in flat 35a,
on Skegoneill Avenue. It's a jumbo box of ghosts built
for old people. We were packed in there by the Housing
Executive when my dad got sacked from the shipyard.
He worked in the pencils department, tried to burn down
a grain store. On the night of the fire, me and mum stood
outside on the Shore Road. I heard boat horns in the dark.
I smelled the hops burn. The working men's club sang.
Dad came home drunk and shouted something like,
Sally, it's a feeling of being cut off, like a star man
capsuled; I am nothing less than drained with worry.
I am all these things at once: short-faced, sorrowful,
useless and blaze-chested. Mum shouted, The mortgage!
Later, she cried on the phone telling granny we had lost
our good, square house facing Crusaders Football Club.
We moved up here to the flat. Dad rarely went out
after that. We had lots of boxes of pencils.

There is a concrete yard out the back of the flats.
Red metal washing poles in rows, no clothes on them.
They stand rusty, out of place, like trees on the moon.
Telephone masts poking out of a duck pond. A sprung black
gate swings shut when men come under the bow-legged
trellis each night. They shout at mum if she walks past
and she says, Oh now. Oh now, I don't like that, boys.
Not in front of the child. I don't invite friends round here
after school. I've a page in my notebook for things found
in the yard. I go out when mum and dad fight.

Last night, I listed eight sun-bleached Guinness cans,
ninety-five small green cubes of busted windscreen glass,
one Star Bar wrapper, an upside-down twin pram.
One foam flying glider – a Curtiss P-40 Tomahawk
in brilliant red, its blue plastic propellor long gone.
There was a small white paper bag, wet and falling apart.
I wrote *pick and mix* in brackets with a question mark.
But it could have held anything. Crumbed ham, or grapes.
Ten Black Jacks. I drew two lines under *pick and mix*?
Brown glossy threads of cassette tape had been wound
around washing poles. I didn't know the right name.
The plastic thing with the spools is a cassette tape,
so the stuff inside can't be cassette tape. I touched my neck
eight times. I drew a picture of a cassette tape. Under it,
I wrote *cassette tape tape*. It went vip-vip in the wind.

Mondays were worst. Hard to be in the world again.
I slept in my uniform, so I only had to wash my face.
It was ten steps from my bedroom door to the bathroom.
I flattened my hair with water and smiled at the mirror.
It made me feel sad. Mum and dad's bedroom door
was open. Mum on the floor, dressing gown untied.
Her nightie was bunched up, she must have been cold.
The blue off-licence bag was stuffed inside a slipper.
It was seven big steps down the hall to the living room.
I edged past my dad, asleep on the brown-striped sofa.
He had been sick on the carpet. My chest might fall open,
I thought. Then it did. I fixed it back six times in a row
by pinching my sternum. Once, again. Once, again.
When it falls open, I hold it together like a split turnip.
I press four fingertips to its left and nip the skin back
over the cleft with the heel of my right hand. Lately,
when the rift begins, I imagine my breastbone fits tight
as a gourd lantern lid. I picture it stitched with toothpicks,
but it won't stay fixed. Two empty cans of Stryke beer
were crumpled up tight, one was balanced on the TV
above the test-card girl, frozen in fright.

It took me a very long time to walk to school.
I had to look at my plimsole shoe soles each step.
I took a step, looked at my sole over my shoulder,
to make sure I hadn't stood in dog's dirt, or gum.
Took a step, looked back again at my sole, no dirt.
It took a hundred and eleven steps to get to Lou's.
Two were really jumps, so I wanted to do it again
when I got to the counter. I inhaled until I was full.
If I filled myself with air I didn't need to go again.
Without looking at me, Lou set down a Dairy Milk
and marked the book.

Seaview Drive is three hundred and seventy-nine steps
to the school steps. At nearly a hundred and fifty-two,
a whippet ran in front of me. It darted from behind a car
into the Hatchet Man's garden. The house was dark blue
in the morning light. Seven crows sat on telephone wires,
one on a lamp post. One bulb was a stuttering pale red,
all the rest threw yellow circles. I started to walk on,
but had lost count. I would have to start the street again.
I inhaled as much air as I could. A bird darted at my head,
looping up and over the roof.

I couldn't see a hatchet in the wild yellow hedge.
The leaves where it sagged in the middle were thin.
A starling fled a bush, skittered up to the guttering.
I crossed the road and stood in front of the house.
The whippet lay on a flat patch of grass in the garden.
I whispered, Do you live here? It didn't reply.
One – two – three – four – I stepped up the path,
crouched by the dog. The crow on the lamp post
flew off with a yawp.

I broke off some chocolate and set it on the grass.
The dog jerked its head to look, lay back down.
Neither windows nor doors slammed open.
Everything felt suddenly very enormous and hot.
I thought about Janet Chowbury's glasses. Too big.
I thought about her navy skirt, which did not fit her.
I thought about Henry Rawley and Shauna Langley.
Kissing and kissing. Lou and the queue and the list.
The thoughts felt sour and pressed against my teeth.
They felt like hard, rough squares rubbing together.
I had to push the quicks down into my fingernails.
I touched my neck eight times and eight times again.
I got out my notebook and wrote, *Owns a whippet,*
a grey one. I underlined it and underlined it.
A voice said, You're the weird wee girl who walks
up and down here and is always late for school.

The Hatchet Man had on blue City Council overalls.
He was talking to me out his living-room window.
I froze in a crouch, leaning on my knee to write.
I waited for grindstone sparks to light up the room.
Woodchip walls and, behind him, an unlit Superser.
His finger shook as he reached to scratch his eyebrow.
Watch yourself, love, there's dog's dirt round here,
he said. There's an awful lot of oul shite everywhere.
He closed the window and pulled the curtains tight.

I never knew what to do when people were kind.
I replayed the echoes of his words in my head
till they went differently. Him asking me,
How many steps in the whole street, Sam?
I would please him by knowing the number.
I'd be the champion because I knew it exact.
He'd say, Tell me your absolute best memories.
And I'd be nine with dad in his work boots
telling a joke. Why are graveyards so popular?
Cos people are dying to get in. I'd say how
his eyes filled up when he laughed. I'd be five
with mum holding my hands above my head
as we dance to Eddy Grant in our sunlit kitchen.
Her wild pale hair a curled halo of light.
Great memories, the Hatchet Man would say.
I pulled open his letter box, pushed my notebook
through the flap with the rest of my chocolate.
Hands over my ears, I counted my heartbeat.
On the street, the lamp posts flickered, went out.
School bell rang. I started my steps from one.

ELLEN

We, Ghost Tigers

Overnight, the last worn-out ripped guddies of summer
tied their own white laces and flung themselves up over
the telephone wires. The wind made them whip and kick,
but they swung tight. The best bit in my favourite film
was when a boy on his own in the woods saw a deer
beside train tracks. It looked at him, then ran into the trees.
No one else saw it. He never told anyone about it.
It was just *his* deer.

It was a month until big school started. The clouds
were dead slow and grey and nearly touched the roofs.
I needed books and shoes and there was no money
until family allowance day at the end of the month.
No mon, no fun, my mum always said. Last week,
I took a twenty from her purse, heavy with coppers.
The note crumpled together with a ripped fiver.
I snuck up Glandore Avenue with it balled up tight
in my fist like a bud. At Billy Duddy's sweet shop,
I cut up the entry. A Harp can was washed of its blue
and dented where it had been worn as a space shoe.
I pulled a lump of stone-dash plaster from the wall
and pressed the twenty into the sodden brickwork.
This morning, the note was still there, looking unreal
in its crack. I took it out and walked home in the rain
as the matchbox houses of Ashfield Gardens lined up
cinnabar, burnt yellow, lint cream and almost blue.

I pushed open the front door, left on the snib. My mum
was in the living room flicking, clicking her long nails,
painted dark hermit purple. The brown wood television
flickered with the sound down. I twisted in the doorway.
Look, I said, holding up the unfurled note. I found money
in the street. Will I go get bread, milk and stuff for tea?
She grinned but didn't answer. She stared at the screen.
The curtains were closed but there I was, a reflected gap
in the window. I love how lucky you are, Ellen, she said.
You're always finding money and saving us. Flick, click.
God must be looking down on you. God must have turned
into a bird and left money on the ground for you to find.
Then her mouth buckled a bit, turned down at one side.
Until bedtime, hushed-up TV people mimed unseen while
she frowned, gasped and disagreed with the wall.

I wandered up to the bright fruit shop by the big church
on the top of Skegoneill Avenue to get a pan loaf, milk,
baked beans, cheese slices, firelighters, crisps, Trios,
Penguins, Rice Krispies and Findus Crispy Pancakes
from the freezer at the back, by the peanut-butter machine.
I asked for a penny sweet but didn't use my own voice.
The man picked a Fizzy Cola Bottle. I pressed my fingertip
against the worn counter. He said, You not from here?
I lied, No, America. He said, Right you are, ten twenty.
I lifted the bag off the counter really fast so it looked
like I was strong and hawked it home. The sour cola fizz
made me cry. My friend Max's dad vanished a week
before this.

I headed out then to meet the gang. I ran down
Fortwilliam Parade's red-brick terrace, brown lintels
and arched door frames. The ladybirds were settled
on nettles as I wriggled on my back under the steel fence
into the Blacky – a still, coarse triangle of wasteland.
Blackberry bush thorns grabbed my T-shirt and shoes.
I stood up on the hill on the other side. Worn trails
like bumpy sutures stitched together bushes, ditches,
a thin river, sparse allotment plots. Worried trees pinned
to the north end hid the edge of Castle High School.
There's meant to be buried caves and a hidden keep.
They cut down a dead man hanging there one time,
the frayed blue rope moved in the willow for years.

A half-burnt sycamore held our unfinished tree hut.
I climbed its kindling ladder, tacked to the trunk,
to wait for Max, Sam and Nell. The building of it
had taken us since Easter and now we would split
to separate schools before it was done. From the start,
I said to Sam the cragged black branch was too high.
It was ten feet up. One similar cracked last winter
onto Glandore Avenue. The rain pooled in its knots
and clefts over days. It lay there forever, rotting.
But here was our hut with its wood pallet floor,
snatched from a Tigers Bay bonfire pile in June.
One wall was nailed branches, another a sheet
of corrugated plastic, cracked. We throw rocks
at allotment sheds balanced on the fence line.
The hut is half-a-house higher than the rooftops.
You can see Skegoneill's Church of the Nazarene.
God did not send His Son to the world to condemn it,
a sign said. You can see Brantwood Football Club,
its locked blue doors, and the bricked-up shell
of Duncairn Homing Pigeon Society. A dull mist
blanket mutes mums and dads and all beneath it.
The base of the tree smells of piss. But up here,
you can see the wind send spoon leaves flying
over the ridge, over that sunken, worn-out
couple of hundred metres of carrots and cabbages
just asking, begging, to be nicked.

Max squeezed under the fence and whacked dirt off
her backside as she walked up the hill in beat-up guddies
and a Gremlins T-shirt where Gizmo looked worried.
She was lost to the world. Hi, I yelled. Your da back yet?
Max shrugged lightly. Something something, she said.
I paused in the middle of chewing my cheek. What?
I want to go find him, she repeated, loudly this time.
I started down the ladder. Max glanced over her shoulder
at the others coming under the fence. Nell and Sam
raised their hands in a wave. See what they think,
she said. The stern sky was a jawbone. Planted in front,
a pitched Land For Sale sign held back a slant of light.

Last week, we were playing hunt in Skegoneill Drive.
Ip dip dog's dick out pops piss. Me and Max split
to hide in Sadie Wilson's gut-pink rhododendron tree
up the back entry. On the way, we grabbed fistfuls
of honeysuckle that grew in bunches moored
over old Elsie's fence. We sat crouched in the mud
sucking fizz dabs of sweet juice, pinching the stems,
biting the bulbs, spitting them out. Max said her dad
didn't come home the night before. I said, Oh yeah?
And she said, Yeah. From nowhere, Sam guldered,
Caught! and we split in a flash up the street.

Next time, Max was It. Sam bolted to the new estate
wired to the bottom of Ashfield. Nell grabbed my wrist
and pulled me over the main road. We jumped the wall
in front of the flats, right beside the bus stop for town,
and a black taxi idling. We crouched on the wet grass.
I rocked back on my heels. I said, Heard you got beat up
round Seaview Drive. Nell blinked at me from one eye,
a purple cantaloupe. Yes, she said. I am bruised. Today,
the wolf pack dandered up the Antrim Road to eat me.
I've had my fill of housing estates. I am wild and ready
to leave. She shifted foot to foot. Nell said, I'm banjaxed.
Her blue eyes shook. I said, Oh, I am banjaxed, too.
She whispered, Let's run away to Woolworths and steal
two whole trays of Fizzy Laces. Apple, cola, I don't care.
A woman at the bus stop shouted over the road to a woman
behind us, Any more shite out of your man, Linda?
She said, I make myself small, Jackie, y'know yourself.

Nell and Sam scuffed up to the black foot of the tree.
Have you checked for your dad in Grove Park?
Nell asked. We knew why she asked. Men died
there every summer and were found swinging by kids
and people cutting through to the big furniture shop
or for Mr Whippy in the Shore Road petrol station.
Someone's mum got beaten and stuffed in a bush once.
Sam said, Are you sure he's not asleep in the house,
or did he go on holiday? Max pulled her top lip down
as far as it went. Could he be lost in town? I asked.
Nell hopped three steps, kicked a stone at the stream.
Sam stared, squeezed her right arm with her left hand.
Max pushed her lip between her teeth and bit down.
Let's check the park first, I said. We squeezed back
under the fence one by one.

It was almost two. We jumped the concrete bollards
down the overgrown lane. We took across Premier Drive
and down the long entry behind Fortwilliam Parade,
overrun with clinging nettles, brambles and puddles.
We ducked a taut washing line stretched from a yard
to a tree. One time, Nell's brother ran straight into it.
He groaned like hurrgh and saw both feet at eye level
as he thrillingly snapped to a halt.

No one spoke as we emerged, darting past traffic
on Skegoneill and down the wide Jellicoe Avenue.
It was long and full of rich houses on one side.
I was skipping there once when a Rottweiler leapt
over a fence and grabbed a blonde girl by the arm.
It shook her and shook her, and a car horn beeped
long flat honks as though that might stop the dog.
Over the street was Grove Park, as wide as the sea,
its green pointed railings forced and bowed into gaps
by kids who had slipped through before us.

Grove Park was a stretched-out, monstrous expanse,
treeless save for a scattering of sycamores shrugged
to the edges. It was like coming to the moon.
We said we'd split into pairs to look for Max's dad,
then meet after in the playground. Me and Nell
watched Max and Sam walk away tilted in the wind
across the huge football pitches to the perimeter.
The peeling clubhouse in Brantwood Football Club
peeked through gaps in the treeline. A dog chained
outside a haunted cuboid council building barked
beneath PRIVATE KEEP OUT signs and razor wire.
There were football boots thrown onto the roof,
joined by knotted laces. One had landed on its studs,
the other on its side. A pile of old wet sand lay
between us and the grass. Nell's cousin Noel told us
about some kid who tunnelled inside. It collapsed on her
and she died. Ten men dug her small body out
after the bookies closed. They left the sand.

You couldn't see from one end of the park to the other. There were no benches for people to wait on or talk at: it was a blueprint for a future park. The freezing wind would jolt you across the vast grass to a flat horizon that fell away to a steep hill. I leant back on the wind like it was a cushion. On your bike, you'd be pushed fast forward until you gushed like Niagara Falls over the line, down a cascade of small hills to the play park. But if you forced yourself to stop at the top, to stand still, to dig your heels, to drop your bike, to bear your hair cutting in your eyes, to feel your unzipped coat buffet and your shirt collar whip your cheeks, you could beat it. You could beat the push, the wind and the endless grass and just stand up before everything lying ahead of you, holding space where grass meets sky, framing the giant harbour beyond.

Nell and I stood staring at the docks. She took my hand.
The clouds were heavy on top of the twin yellow cranes.
Parked cruise ships, grain tanks, blue metal outhouses,
Thompson's animal feed mill, curved white plastic roofs,
small pink derricks, the burnt red-brick Jennymount Mill
at North Derby Street, chimneys, big waste pipe pointed
at the sky, Sinclair Seamen's Church spire peeking out
on the dark corner of Sailortown. The headstrong smell
that blew across, up and through, framing everything:
the stuck salt from the Irish Sea mixed with the fixed
rivet musk of the feed. Round the corner, you land down
the York Road on top of Gallaher's cigarette factory
and because of it the whole city smoked.

Max wound towards us on the thin perimeter path.
She waved at me and Nell. Spitting rain started.
I shouted, Where's Sam? Max pointed behind her.
Sam was taking slow, careful steps in our direction
out of the scribbled sycamores, promising life.
She looked up, shouted. The wind grabbed it away.

He's not here, Max said. Let's just go look in town.
She knew the city as her aunt worked in Primark
and took her with her on the bus on Saturdays
past the spaceship red and black buoy fountains.
Max would sit all day on a stool in the fitting room
as people tried clothes and left them scattered.
In a bomb scare last week, people dropped socks
and pants crowding out the Castle Street door.
I got lost in the town looking for my dropped Lego.
A stranger took my hand near the Albert Clock.
He smiled and said, Mon on here, you, with me.
I said, No, and shouted, No. I pulled and yanked.
A hairdresser called Viv took me home in her car.
Near my street, I was scared she'd see where I lived
and find out my mum stared, so I jumped out
at the traffic lights and ran through a cloud of wasps
taking sacramental grace by a bin.

Let's check in the bush hut, I said. Just in case.
They knew what I meant. We had built it at Easter
down the front of the park beyond the playground.
It overlooked York Road, its colossal bible signs
at the bus stop telling us, NOW IS THE ACCEPTED TIME.
We forgot the bush hut since starting the tree hut.
I'd left *Beano*, *Beezer* and *Dandy* comics inside.
In between us and there, the Red Fang gang
sat on the rubber swings, smoking and spitting.
Their leader was from the new Ashfield Gardens.
He was Ryan Coyle, who ran at me one time
as I was playing cribby, his crazy face teetering,
shouting, Spurs are at the bottom of the league!
I said, I know. But he meant my zip was down.
He punched my face. A different time, his mum
threw a six-pack of Tennent's at our bay window
and the glass was even in my cup of juice.

Max rubbed her face, looked at me. Let's just go,
she said. Forget it. Hundreds of swallows tripped
and fell and rose over the grass, like the blue tattoo
on Max's dad's arm. When I called for her to play,
he would stand on the stairs. Maxine, he'd say.
If I hear you've been hanging about with taigs,
I'll skelp your hole. She'd swerve past out the door
like he was made of spikes. He would shout,
D'ya hear me? After her. D'ya hear me? Wee cunt.
We walked to Skegoneill bus stop in single file.

I knew every summer when it was the heat's last day.
There was a smell. It started to spit as light bounced
off the windows of the flats. It seemed more beautiful
because now it would lash for a month. I knew last year
when Nell and I were walking up Skegoneill in the rain,
laughing, our arms around each other's shoulders,
singing the wrong words of Noo York, Noo York.
Start dreading the loos, I'm Stevie Bublé. I want to –

Funny enough, my dad went yellow right after Nell's.
There must have been a cancer wind blowing around.
Mum had said it was obvious he would die in the hospice
on Somerton Road and she hoped it was AIDS in fact
and he deserved it as he didn't pay child maintenance
except 10p, which was the minimum. I should hate him,
she said. And if I didn't, she would give me away.
The video shop man always said my dad spat me out.

Nell cupped her ear at the bus turning weightless
around the Glandore roundabout. Rain fell harder.
The brakes on the red 64 Downview hissed.
Let's go, she said, before the whole day breaks us!
Sam clapped, Yeah! As the shivering bus stopped,
I heard myself think, This day is beautiful.
In star jumps we passed through its pleated doors
and past the driver up the wet, grubby gangway.
The worn black wall of Brantwood Football Club
disappeared on our right as the bus shunted off,
pitching down majestic Skegoneill Avenue.
Then past the library, warm lights, wide windows,
where we'd sit with legs crossed on worn carpet
reading ghost books until we had to go home.
We swung right onto York Road. The fixed metal
billboards with the Lord's Word nailed on stilts
passed over our heads. In Glasgow Street, queer kids
threw stones and milk bottles at cars as they passed.
We slipped by the glorious marble Grove Baths.
Nell, Sam and Max were discussing the Hatchet Man
and new schools. I let my eyes drift out the window
to Grove Park's pickle-green railings and hedge
made of hornbeam. Behind them, our old bush hut
lit by a spotlight glow, and for a second it was just
my deer, like the one in the film. No one else saw it.
I thought Max's dad might be in there reading comics.
He might be OK. He might be shouting, Go on, girls,
right youse are! Everything's going to be all right.

ACKNOWLEDGEMENTS

Thank you to the editors of *Still Worlds Turning* (No Alibis Press) and *Belfast Stories* (Doire Press), where some of this writing first appeared in an earlier form. I am grateful for the support of the Arts and Humanities Research Council (via the Northern Bridge Doctoral Training Partnership) for funding and developmental support.

Thank you to the awesome Rachael Allen. I'm indebted to the team at Granta Books for their extraordinary care and attention in bringing this book to life. Thank you to Leontia Flynn for the push to step unafraid into Belfast. Thanks to Gail McConnell for much bolstering and wisdom. For every support I am grateful to Queen's University staff, past and present, including Fran Brearton, Ian Sansom, Stephen Kelly, Stephen Sexton, Philip McGowan, Glenn Patterson and Ramona Wray. Thanks to Philippa Sitters at DGA. Thank you, always, to Prof. Ciaran Carson for showing me a way to begin to walk these streets.

I'm grateful to friends and family for their encouragement: Mícheál McCann, Hilary McCollum, Arlene Hand, Scott McKendry, Duane Roberts, Mervyn Marshall, Lauren Swiney and Kelsie Donnelly. Thank you to Stephani Dempsey for always being on the bleachers. I am forever thankful for the beautiful people that are my brother and sister, James Watson and Tanya Hefer-Watson. Thanks to Deby McKnight for the sausage rolls and helping me navigate this landscape. Thank you to my amazing son Art for showing me another, more epic, way to be twelve. Thank you to my wife, and first reader, Sarah, for making it possible to write this. Actually, for making everything possible.